The Little Fir Tree

Margaret Wise Brown

pictures by

Jim LaMarche

HARPERCOLLINSPUBLISHERS

A little fir tree stood by the edge of a forest, a little way off from the great green trees.

It had been a windy day the day the little fir tree was a seed, and he had blown through the air, out of the forest and into the field. And there he had dropped to the ground.

As Spring and Summer and Autumn and Winter passed by and another Spring turned green, the little seed had sprouted, taken root, and grown.

Seven times the Spring had come flashing with birds and flowers.

Seven times the Summer had droned its hot bee-buzzing days around him. Seven Autumns had whirled their falling leaves and milkweed parachutes past his head. And now the snow fell and the grasses of the fields crackled with the diamond light of ice.

His seventh Winter had come.

Always the little fir tree looked over at the big fir trees in the great dark forest. He felt a little lonesome in his littleness, away from the other trees. He wished he were part of the forest or part of something, instead of growing all alone out there, a little fir tree in a big empty field.

One day a man came out of the forest. He carried a shovel and wore long black boots.

He walked right up to the little fir tree and he gave him a shake.

"Not too little and not too big,
Not too stiff nor yet too limber,
A beautiful little green fir tree,
Just the tree for my boy to grow
strong with."

So—tenderly the man dug into the not-quite-frozen ground.
He dug a big wide hole around the little fir tree. Tenderly he
took all the far-flung roots and tied them in a gunnysack.

Then he lifted the little fir tree high in the air and proudly he
bore him through the forest.

"You are going to a great Celebration," said the man, "and you will be a part of it. Then in the early Spring I will bring you back and plant you again where I found you. Each year you will return to the great Celebration and each year you will go back to your own green field in the Spring.

"And you will grow with my little boy who cannot come to you. You shall be his living tree."

For the little boy had a lame leg. He had never been in the forest. He had never left his bed. But he listened to the trees at night, and he watched the trees beyond his windows, the great green trees he saw in the distance: and he wished for a tree that would come to him.

Now one was coming, borne on his father's shoulders through the forest. The little fir tree was coming, with a swish of branches and a prickly green smell.

It was planted in a great wooden tub at the foot of the boy's bed.
"You have come to me from the wild green forest," said the
little boy. "And you are a part of my very own world. You have
come to the great Celebration of Christmas."

The next night candles were lit in the windows and outside the snow fell softly and covered the trees with white. But inside the house the little fir tree was green, and pungent, and warm.

Then they put golden tinsel on his branches

And golden bells

And green icicles

And silver stars

And red and green and blue and purple chains of shining Christmas balls.

And soon—o shining wonder—the little fir tree was . . .

A CHRISTMAS TREE

Children came that night to sing Christmas carols. They sang new words to an old carol that the boy had made up in the joy of the day:

> *O Christmas Tree,*
> *O Christmas Tree!*
> *Your greenest branches*
> *Live for me.*

After Winter, Spring came in,
flashing with birds and flowers,
and the little fir tree was returned
to the woods.

Summer droned
its bee-buzzing days
around him.

And Autumn came and
whirled milkweed parachutes
past his head.

But when snow fell still and white over the fields, heavy and silent on the forest, the time had come for the little fir tree to be carried once more to the bright lights of the Celebration.

And it happened. The man in long boots came and carried him back to the little boy.

Both the boy and the tree were a little bigger. And the lights seemed even brighter. And again the children came.

Again they sang Christmas carols and the song they had sung before. Again they sang the new words to the old, old tune and they sang and they sang them to the living tree.

All Winter long the little fir tree grew
in the little boy's window. Then one gentle day
the wind blew warm and the pussy willows
bloomed. And the boy's father shouldered
the tree and returned with him to the field at
the edge of the woods.

The tree was growing fast now. Little flowers had sprung up around him, making a young and feathery forest at his feet.

Spring warmed into Summer.

And Summer droned into
the crisper sounds of Autumn.

Snow fell early;
it fell soft and deep.

The little fir tree dreamed away and waited for the time the man in black boots would come and get him.

But the man did not come.

More snow fell. And then it stopped snowing and the air was vast and still and very quiet. But the man did not come. The sun shone down and the stars shone down and no one came. There he was, a little fir tree in a big empty field. The big trees in the great dark forest were far away. The stars were far away.

And without Christmas the world seemed big and cold and empty.

Then in the white and snowy darkness he heard singing. Far off, he heard the Christmas carols, across the frozen fields.

The music grew louder and, joy of joys, it came nearer.
And there, leading the dark band of carolers across the
snow, with a lantern in his hand, came the little boy. He was
WALKING, walking out to his tree near the forest.

They came and decked the tree with the shining splendor of tinsel, and hung red berries and apples and cookies on his branches for the birds to eat.

And they sang the song they had sung before:

     O Christmas Tree,
     O Christmas Tree!
     Your greenest branches
     Live for me.

In memory of Ernie Pinamonti
—J.L.M.

The Little Fir Tree   Text copyright © 1954 by Roberta Rauch and Bruce Bliven, Jr.   Text copyright renewed 1982 by Roberta Brown Rauch   Illustrations copyright © 2005 by Jim LaMarche   Manufactured in China. All rights reserved.
www.harperchildrens.com

Library of Congress Cataloging-in-Publication Data
Brown, Margaret Wise.   The little fir tree. Pictures by Jim LaMarche. p.   cm.
Summary: A lonely little fir tree, standing by itself at the edge of the forest, has its life transformed when a father comes and digs it up and takes it home to serve as a living Christmas tree for his bedridden son.
ISBN 0-06-028189-8 — 0-06-028190-1 (lib. bdg.)   [1. Fir—Fiction.   2. Christmas trees—Fiction.]
PZ7.B8163 Lhg   2004   54005535
[E]—dc21   CIP   AC

Typography by Al Cetta   3   4   5   6   7   8   9   10   ❖   First Edition

A hardcover edition of this book was published in 1954 by Crowell.